WE LISTEN TO OUR BODIES

Lydia Bowers

Illustrated by Isabel Muñoz

With Song from
Peaceful Schools

We say what's OKAY

free spirit
PUBLISHING®

Library of Congress Cataloging-in-Publication Data
Names: Bowers, Lydia, author. | Muñoz, Isabel, illustrator.
Title: We listen to our bodies / Lydia Bowers ; illustrated by Isabel Muñoz.
Description: Minneapolis, MN : Free Spirit Publishing, [2021] | Series: We say what's okay | Audience: Ages 3–5
Identifiers: LCCN 2020022501 | ISBN 9781631985003 (hardcover) | ISBN 9781631985010 (pdf) | ISBN 9781631985027 (epub)
Subjects: LCSH: Senses and sensation in children—Juvenile literature. | Emotions in children—Juvenile literature | Perception in children—
    Juvenile literature. | Human body—Juvenile literature.
Classification: LCC BF723.S35 B69 2021 | DDC 152.1/88—dc23
LC record available at https://lccn.loc.gov/2020022501

Edited by Christine Zuchora-Walske
Cover and interior design by Shannon Pourciau

Printed in China

Free Spirit Publishing
An imprint of Teacher Created Materials
9850 51st Avenue North, Suite 100
Minneapolis, MN 55442
(612) 338-2068
help4kids@freespirit.com
freespirit.com

DEDICATION

To the real-life people behind the characters in my stories,
who make the world so much more interesting.

Sami and Harrison, you are the reason I wanted to write children's books.

Jared, you always believed I could do this. I love you.

Mom gave Deja a quick hug and nudged her into the classroom.

Rushed mornings like this made Deja's arms feel shivery. Her eyes felt like crying.

She wanted to hug Mom again. But Mom was already walking away.

Ms. H called out, "The weather is beautiful! Let's head to the playground, everyone!" Deja's feet felt antsy. She loved playing outside.

On the playground Deja shouted to her friend, "Try to catch me, Jackson!" She took off. She was a fast runner, but so was Jackson. He chased her under the climber and around the sandbox. They laughed and dodged their friends as they ran.

Jackson ran closer. Deja's heart pounded harder.
She still laughed, but her face felt hot.
Her eyes felt wet. Her arms felt shivery again.

As Jackson reached out to tag her, Deja whirled around and shoved him away.
He fell hard on the ground. So did Deja. She burst into tears. Then Jackson did too.

Mr. B rolled over in his wheelchair. "Oh, it looks like you had a collision!"
He offered each child a hand as they stood up.

Deja felt her whole body shaking. She knew she shouldn't push.
She had done it without thinking. She worried that Mr. B was angry with her.

Instead, he held her hand and asked, "Deja, how is your body feeling right now? It looks like a lot of feelings are happening."

Deja took a big, hiccup-y breath. She gasped, "I'm shaky and cry-y."

Mr. B nodded. He said, "Even though you were laughing, your face looked scared."

"I'm not scared of tag!" Deja said.

"That's true," agreed Mr B. "I know you like to play tag with your friends. But we have to check in with our bodies to see what they're telling us."

"My body can't talk!" Deja replied.

"Well, no, our bodies don't talk like you and I are talking. They talk in different ways. When you feel shaky or cry-y, your body might be saying, 'Deja! Something's wrong!'" Deja giggled at Mr. B's silly voice. "But listening to our bodies takes practice."

Back inside, Mr. B gathered the children for circle time.
He asked them each to find one thing in the classroom they
really liked and bring it to the group. Deja brought a smooth
river stone from the science table. It felt cool and slippery in her hand.

Mr. B nodded. "Our bodies send us messages. Your bodies are sending different messages about the shoes, and that's okay! Harrison's body tells him he likes to wear the shoes. Deja's body tells her she's worried about falling."

Jackson called out, "When I hear a dog barking, I feel worried."

"Oh yeah?" said Mr. B. "How do you know you're feeling worried?"

Mr. B smiled. "How does your body feel when you wear them?"

Harrison thought for a moment and said, "My feet feel happy! Like jumping!"

Deja declared, "I don't like those shoes. My eyes say the sparkles are pretty, but my feet say, 'No way, I don't want to fall!'"

"Your body looks calm and relaxed," Mr. B said. Deja nodded.
"Harrison, what about you?"

Harrison held up some high-heeled, glittery purple dress-up shoes. "I love these shoes!
They make sparkles on the walls!" He slipped them on his feet. "And they go tap-tap-tap
like this!" He walked across the room.

Mr. B said, "Deja, what did you find?" Deja opened her hand to reveal the stone. Mr. B smiled. "How does your body feel when you hold that?"

Deja thought for a moment. "My body feels like . . ." and she gave a big sigh. She dropped her arms to her sides and smiled.

"My head goes like this!" Jackson put his hands on his cheeks and shook his head back and forth.

"I feel worried in my face," said Harrison. He scrunched his face into little crinkles.

"What about you, Deja?" asked Mr. B. "How does your body feel worried?"

Deja remembered how she felt playing tag. "I feel shaky all over, and my eyes are cry-y."

"When our bodies feel worried, it might mean we need something. Or maybe there's danger nearby. It can be confusing. It's okay to ask a grown-up you trust for help."

"How does your body tell you it's safe and happy?" asked Mr. B.

Jackson said, "My baby sister kicks her feet and makes drool bubbles.
My dads say it's because she's happy to see me."

Deja scrunched up her nose. "My happy doesn't feel like drool bubbles!"

The children giggled and made bubbling noises.

As the children left circle time to play, Mr. B called Deja over. He said, "I noticed your morning seemed a little rushed." Deja nodded. "Sometimes when we are in a hurry, we might not listen to our bodies."

Deja felt her eyes get cry-y again. "I'm listening now.
My body says it feels sad. I miss my mom.
I want to hug her."

Mr. B nodded. He said, "I know teacher hugs
aren't the same as mom hugs.
What could we do to help you feel safe until
you can get a mom hug?"

"How about a teacher hug *and* we read some books?" said Deja.

Mr. B replied, "Good idea! I know that would make me feel happy!"

Deja nodded, "But no drool bubbles!"

Mr. B smiled. "Deal."

CONSENT: A GUIDE FOR CARING ADULTS

CONSENT FOUNDATIONS

What Is Consent?

Consent is a nuanced concept. Its meaning expands as children and situations mature. With young children, we can use the definition *agreeing because you want to*. This child-friendly definition inspired the series title We Say What's Okay.

Why Consent?

As high-profile assault allegations and hidden abuse have come to light in recent years, more and more people have called for the need to teach about consent. These conversations tend to focus on high schools, colleges, and places of employment. However, they need to happen much earlier to be the most effective—just as it is important to read to young children and give them opportunities to run and play to support cognitive and physical development. Consent is a social and emotional skill that requires learning and practice. Caring adults can help children build the foundations of consent early on.

Consent is a principle that we as adults can practice in our lives and model for children. When we create a culture of consent, we provide a safe space for children and empower them to have a voice. This guide offers help in that effort. It is not just a one-time lesson plan. This is ongoing work. The more we and the children in our care practice trusting our instincts and saying no when something feels off in the day-to-day, the more likely we are to trust ourselves when we are in danger. When we as parents, teachers, social workers, and caregivers can make our spaces safe, consensual, and communicative, children know that they can come to us for support.

The Fallacy of Stranger Danger

Of children who are sexually abused, 93 percent are abused by someone they know.* Saying no to someone you know and trust can be difficult, but it is a vital skill. We need to empower children to say no at home and in other familiar, day-to-day environments. It is not children's job to protect themselves from abuse. That is our job. But we can use consent foundations to empower children and to mitigate risk.

Five Steps for Teaching Consent

Building consent foundations involves teaching children five key concepts:

- I listen to my body.
- I am in charge of my body.
- I ask permission.
- I check in.
- I accept no.

---

* RAINN. 2020. "Child Sexual Abuse." rainn.org/articles/child-sexual-abuse.

PHYSICAL AND EMOTIONAL AWARENESS

Listening to Our Bodies

This book can help you teach children about the first concept: listening to our bodies. We humans tend to not listen to our bodies. We often push our feelings aside or say things like "I have no reason to feel like this!" We want to look for evidence to support our feelings, and we do not always trust our gut reactions.

But there *is* scientific evidence for trusting our gut reactions. The vagus nerve is the largest nerve in the body. It stretches from the brain through the torso, and its branches wrap around many of our organs. The vagus nerve and the brain constantly send messages back and forth. Our brain takes in information from our organs and makes decisions about our physical responses before we even realize it. If our brain feels we may be in danger, it tells the vagus nerve to alert our bodies: we may tense up, or the hairs on our arms rise, or our stomach clenches. Even when we are not in danger, our body is still sending us messages. Talk with children about the sensations Deja felt. Have you ever felt some of those feelings? What do you think your body was trying to tell you?

Unfortunately, we often just ignore all our body's warnings. We may say yes to something when we feel uncomfortable about it.

When we listen to our bodies, we notice our body's response to a situation. We think about why we feel that way. Let's say a relative wants to hug you and reaches their arms toward you. You feel your body tense up. Listening to your body means noticing that tension and thinking about it. Maybe you don't want to hug your relative because you just feel touched out. Maybe you don't want to hug this person because they don't feel safe to you. Now let's say a relative reaches out for a hug and your body feels relief or joy. Your body might be telling you that you do want a hug because you need physical connection with someone who cares about you.

Trauma note: When we have experienced trauma, it may be challenging to make sense of our body's responses. Sometimes alerts from our brain may get communicated as "THIS IS NOT A DRILL! ALL HANDS ON DECK! GO! GO! GO!" The vagus nerve tells our lungs to tighten. We feel dizzy from lack of oxygen, we start breathing heavily, our whole body is tense and on edge, and we end up in a panic attack. When our bodies respond to trauma triggers or to chronic stress, we often experience a "fight, flight, or freeze" response. As adults, we may want to try to rationally talk through what's happening with a child. But because they are in

survival mode, their heart rate is up, their senses are sharper (and may be in overload), and their breathing is heavier—and the logical, thinking, learning part of their brain is not in control at the moment.

Recognizing Emotions

Recognizing emotions can be tricky. Sometimes we must start small, and simply notice pleasure in moments like a breeze on our skin or a warm hug. Deja enjoyed the feel of the smooth stone, and Harrison liked the sparkles and clicking noise of the dress-up shoes. When we are able to say "I like this hug because it feels warm and it makes a happy feeling in my chest," then we are better able to recognize a contrasting emotion: "This hug does not give me that same happy feeling, but gives me an achy feeling in my stomach."

Trauma note: Traumatized children may feel panic and anxiety in moments of calm and quiet, because they do not know when the next bad thing will happen—but they know it is inevitable. And the moment something bad does happen—even if it is a caregiver getting upset—then they feel relief, thinking *this is familiar*. As safe adults, we must make sure we are watching and talking through those moments—speaking truth into the confusion and panic.

Activities
What Feels Good?

Have children find one or two objects that they like, just as the children in this book do. If children need more explanation, ask them, "What is something that makes you feel happy? Maybe it's something with a smell, sound, or texture you like. Maybe it reminds you of something good." Talk about the objects together. The idea is to connect the tangible (this object) to the intangible (this feeling or emotion). Note that different people may have different responses to different objects. We like different things, which is okay. You can also have children do the opposite: find something they do not like. Talk about those objects and feelings as well.

This activity can help children not only identify feelings, but also build empathy. A key element of empathy is considering how someone else feels. For example: "I don't understand why you hate glitter.

But maybe the way you feel about glitter is the way I feel about slime. (Ew! Gross!)" The concept of putting yourself in someone else's shoes is much easier to grasp if it it's connected to tangible, physical responses.

Emotions Body Map

Part of learning to listen to our bodies is identifying how our emotions and feelings manifest physically. We can do this by making an emotions body map. You can use a large roll of paper to make a life-size outline of each child, or use smaller sheets of paper. Many researchers agree that there are six basic human emotions found in every culture around the globe: anger, surprise, joy, disgust, sadness, and fear. Choose a color to represent each emotion, such as:

anger = red

surprise = orange

joy = yellow

disgust = green

sadness = blue

fear = purple

Go through the emotions one by one with the children, and identify where in your body you feel that emotion. When you feel angry, do you tighten up your fists? Color your hands red! When you are happy, do you run and jump? Color your feet yellow! We do not all feel things the same way. For some, fear may be goosebumps on their arms. For others, fear may be a sick feeling in their stomach.

As you do this activity, you may notice that feelings often manifest in the torso. (There's that vagus nerve in action!) You may also notice that emotions, like colors, may overlap and blend. Check out the book *I'm Happy-Sad Today* by Lory Britain for a fun story (and more resources) on mixed-together emotions.

Sing a Song About Listening to Our Bodies

In addition to identifying how feelings show up physically, you can also use the song "We Listen to Our Bodies" by Peaceful Schools on the next page. The lyrics remind us to check in with our bodies. Our bodies send us messages about our emotions!

Recommended Books and Websites

Books

Britain, Lory. 2019. *I'm Happy-Sad Today*. Minneapolis, MN: Free Spirit Publishing.

Garcia, Gabi. 2017. *Listening to My Body*. Austin, TX: Skinned Knee Publishing.

Kurtzman-Counter, Samantha, and Abbie Schiller. 2014. *Miles Is the Boss of His Body*. Santa Monica, CA: The Mother Company.

Morrison, Eleanor. 2018. *C Is for Consent*. Los Angeles: Phonics with Finn.

Websites

Child Mind Institute. childmind.org.

Educate2Empower Publishing. e2epublishing.info.

National Association for the Education of Young Children (NAEYC): Social and Emotional Development. naeyc.org/resources/topics/social-and-emotional-development.

National Child Traumatic Stress Network nctsn.org.

Sex Positive Families. sexpositivefamilies.com.

WE LISTEN TO OUR BODIES

Music by Shawn Forster • Lyrics by Shawn Forster and Beth Amuso • © 2020 by Peaceful Schools

You can hear a recording of this song at freespirit.com/song.

(CHORUS)

We lis - ten to our bo - dies, let's

prac - tice what to do. Our

bo - dies send us mes - sa - ges, trust your -

self to help you through.

Is your body feeling shaky?
There may be something wrong.
Are you feeling antsy? Your heart's pounding?
Maybe you're not feeling strong.
Does your face feel hot?
Feel a shiver up your spine?
Listening to our bodies
Helps us each and every time.

CHORUS

Is your body feeling calm?
That tells us something too.
Are you feeling happy? You're relaxed?

The smile on your face can be a clue.
Are you feeling peaceful?
When you feel safe, that's a sign!
Listening to our bodies
Helps us each and every time.

CHORUS

Check in with your body and see what it says.
It can tell us when we're safe or when danger is nearby.
The message can be clear or confusing at times.
Ask a grown-up you trust if you need help to decide.

CHORUS

ABOUT THE AUTHOR AND ILLUSTRATOR

Lydia Bowers is a speaker, consultant, and trainer who happily exists in the Venn diagram overlap between early childhood and sex education. After spending almost two decades of working directly with children as a classroom teacher and a parent, she is passionate about reframing sexuality conversations. Lydia now teaches families and educators how to talk to children about subjects like gender, reproduction, and abuse. When she's not traveling around the country for conferences and speaking engagements, she lives in Cincinnati with her husband and two children and adds to her growing collection of children's book character tattoos as often as she can.

Isabel Muñoz's dream was to paint for a living, and now she's proud to be the illustrator of several children's books. She works from a tiny and colorful studio in the north of Spain. You can follow her work at isabelmg.com.